Bob
and the Big Plan

Wendy
and the Surprise Party

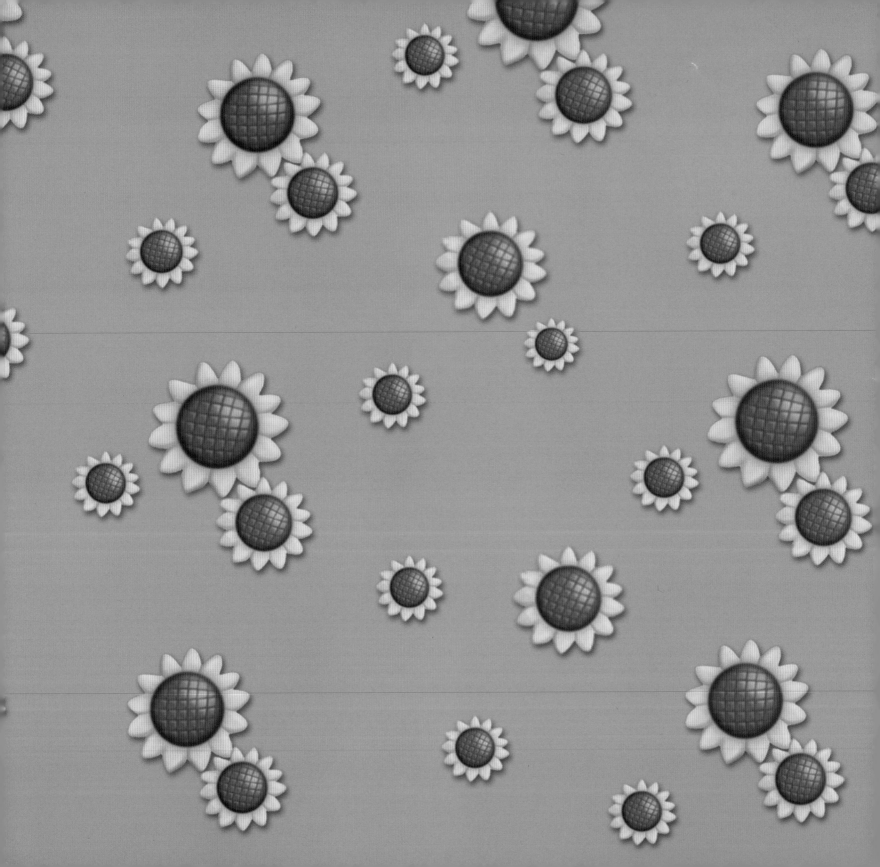

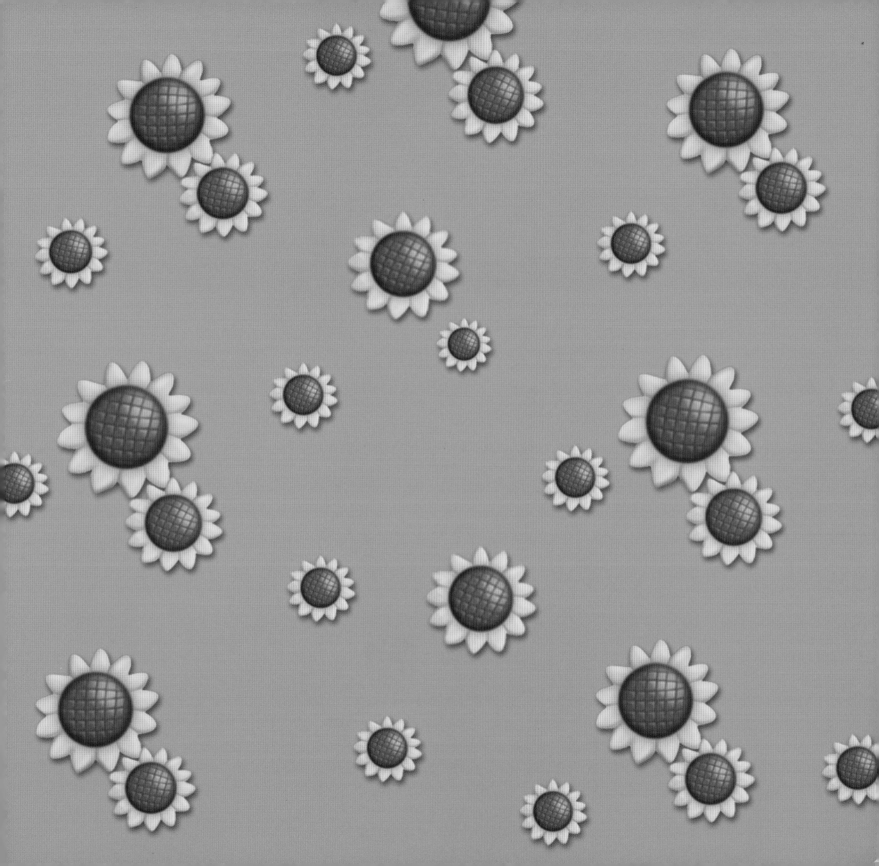

EGMONT

We bring stories to life

This edition published for BCA in 2008
First published in Great Britain 2007
by Egmont UK Limited,
239 Kensington High Street, London W8 6SA

HiT entertainment

ISBN 978 0 6035 6378 2

1 3 5 7 9 10 8 6 4 2
Printed in Italy

CONTENTS

Bob
and the Big Plan

Wendy
and the Surprise Party

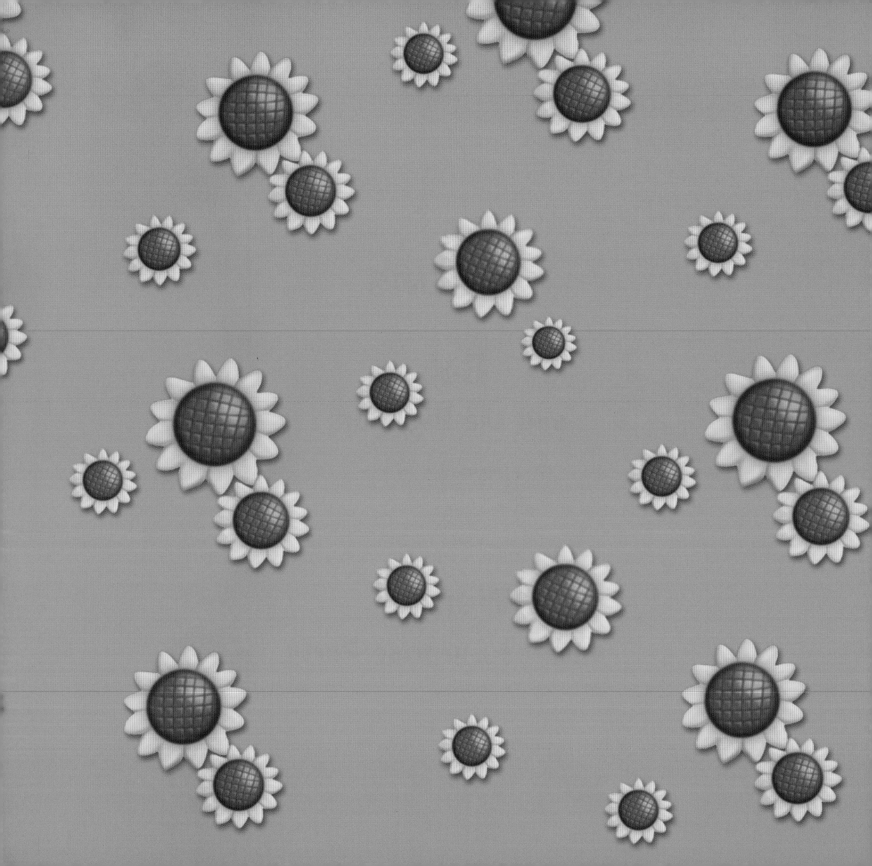

Bob
and the Big Plan

Illustrations by Craig Cameron

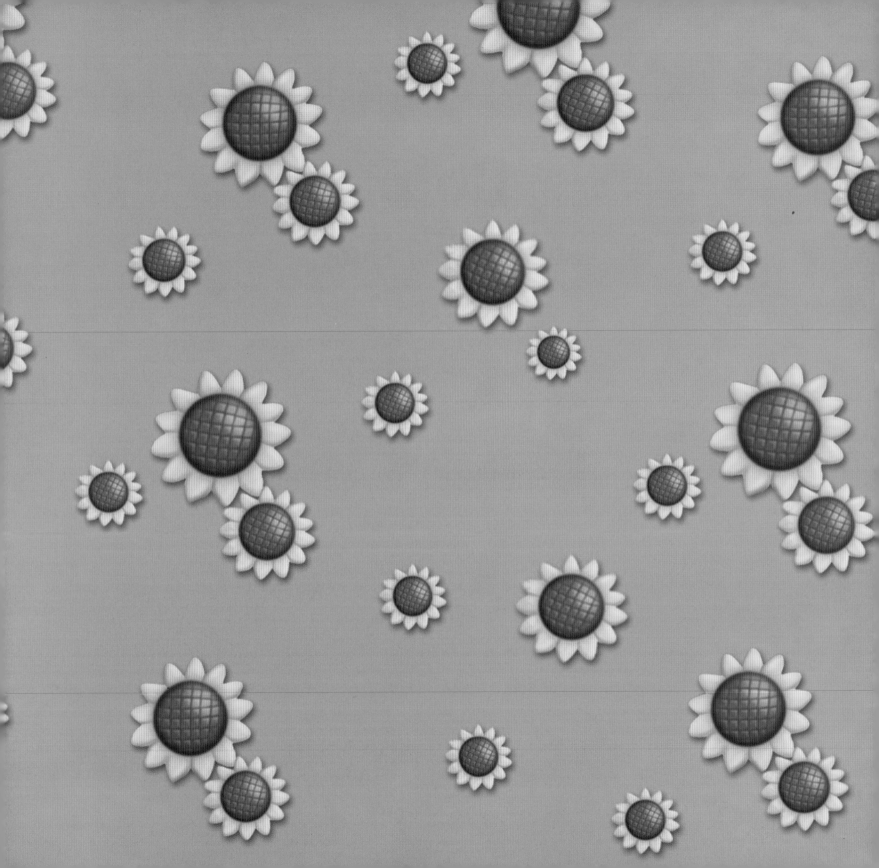

When Bob hears about
a competition to build
Sunflower Valley, he faces
his biggest building challenge
yet. He's going to need
a Big Plan ...

Bob and the team were busy at work, building
a bigger office for Mr Adams the architect.

"I'll need more space if I win the competition
to plan a new town in Sunflower Valley,"
Mr Adams explained. "I've been working on
my model for weeks!"

"We used to go to Sunflower Valley on holiday
when I was young!" said Bob.

But Bob felt sad when he saw the model.
Mr Adams had turned Sunflower Valley
into a noisy city, packed with busy roads
and big buildings.

"I'm taking this to the town hall, so everyone
can have a good look," said Mr Adams.
"The judging is the day after tomorrow.
Goodbye, Bob!"

"Why don't you enter the competition, Bob?" asked Muck, later on.

"Great idea!" said Dizzy.

"Ho, ho! I'm a builder, not an architect like Mr Adams," said Bob. "And I have lots of work to do here."

Dizzy and Muck were disappointed. But the next morning, Bob changed his mind. He didn't want Sunflower Valley to be spoiled.

"What about the job here, Bob?" asked Scoop, sounding worried.

"Can you finish the foundations by yourselves?" said Bob. "The competition is tomorrow!"

"Can we build it?" said Scoop.

"Yes, we can!" chimed Roley and Muck.

"Er, yeah, I think so," added Lofty.

Back at the yard, Bob was looking through his books for ideas.

"Wow! Look at these buildings, Pilchard," said Bob. "I'll need a Big Plan to win this competition!"

"Miaow!" said Pilchard.

Later, Roley and Bird were watching Bob sketch his ideas for Sunflower Valley. But when Bob drew houses, they didn't look right.

"Toot, toot!" squawked Bird. He was showing Bob his nest.

"Good idea, Bird!" smiled Bob. "I'll have houses that don't spoil the countryside, like yours!"

"Brilliant!" said Roley.

Bob had almost finished his model, when he heard a noise outside. Vrrooom! Vrrooom!

Just then, Mr Bentley appeared on a shiny off-road vehicle. "Hello, Bob," he said. "I'm just taking Scrambler to the town hall – he's part of the prize for the competition!"

"Nice to meet you, Scrambler!" smiled Bob.

At Mr Adams' office, the team was in trouble. Dizzy was pouring out cement for the foundations, when Scoop noticed the markers were in the wrong place. Concrete spilled everywhere!

"Oh, no! What are we going to do?" worried Scoop.

"We'll have to fetch Bob before the concrete goes hard!" said Muck.

"We're really sorry, Bob," said Muck, when Bob arrived. "We made a mistake!"

"Now you won't have time to finish your model," sighed Dizzy.

"If we work quickly, we can move the concrete before it sets and use it later," said Bob, kindly.

"Reduce, reuse, recycle!" said the team. And they worked together until the job was done.

Bob had just arrived back in the yard when, suddenly, the lights went out.

"It's a power cut!" said Bob. "Fetch some lamps, Muck."

While Bob finished his model, he told the machines about the different ways to make power. "We'll use the sun and the wind to power Sunflower Valley!" he said.

"Wind turbines and solar panels! How cool!" said Scoop, excitedly.

The next day at the town hall, Mr Adams was finishing his speech when Bob appeared.

"Wait!" shouted Bob. "Here's my Big Plan for Sunflower Valley! We'd use recycled things to build a beautiful town," he explained. "Everything would be powered by water, wind and sun to save energy!"

"Ooh!" and "Wow!" went the crowd, when they saw Bob's model.

The judges looked at both models and nodded their heads.

"It gives me great pleasure to declare the winner and present him with Scrambler.
It's . . . Bob the Builder!" said the Mayoress.

"We hope you'll plan and build Sunflower Valley!" said a judge.

Bob was very happy. "Welcome to the team, Scrambler!" he smiled. "Sunflower Valley, here we come!"

THE END

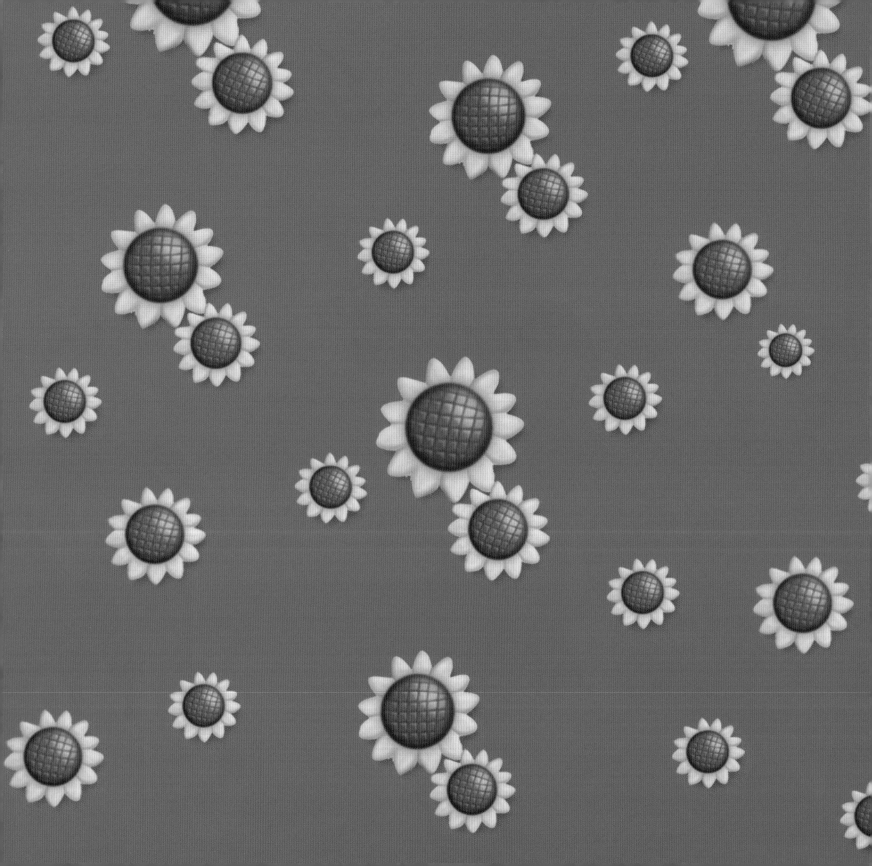

Wendy
and the Surprise Party

Illustrations by Pulsar

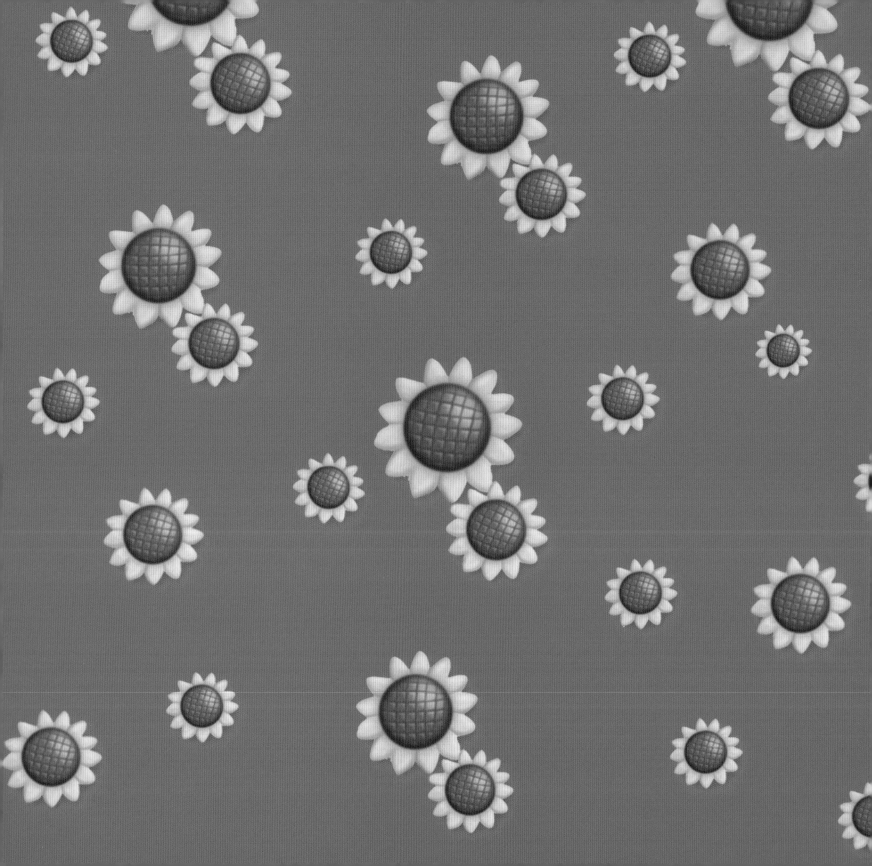

When Wendy planned a surprise party for Bob, she had to organise the dome building work at the same time! Would Wendy be able to do both?

In Sunflower Valley, Bob and the team were building a dome.

"You've done a great job getting all the parts, Wendy," said Bob. "So I think you should be in charge."

" Oh Bob, I'd love to!" replied Wendy. But then she began to look worried.

As Bob walked away, Wendy whispered to the machines:

"I need you to help me keep Bob busy. I'm planning a surprise party for him tomorrow night at the dome! Mr Bentley is letting everyone know."

"But the dome isn't built yet!" cried Muck.

Wendy wasn't worried about building the dome. But she was worried about how she was going to organise the party! Bob and the machines were ready to start.

"Can we build it?" asked Scoop.

"Yes we can!" replied the machines.

"Er . . . yeah, I think so," added Lofty.

They dug the foundations and made a timber frame.

Then Scrambler whizzed in with Mr and Mrs Bentley.

"Hello, everybody!" said Mr Bentley.
"We are here to pick a spot for our new house!"

"We're going to live in a tent while we build it," added Mrs Bentley.

"I'll show you where to pitch it," offered Wendy. But she was really leaving so she could organise the party!

Wendy had just picked up her phone when Scoop arrived.

"Can you come back and tell Bob what to do next?"
asked Scoop.

"Bernard will help you with the party tonight,"
said Mrs Bentley.

"Tonight?" replied Wendy. "But the party is tomorrow!"

Mr Bentley had told everyone to come on the wrong night! Wendy decided that she would organise the party when she got back from the building site.

"We've got to be quick or it won't be finished in time," said Wendy, when she saw Bob and Dizzy stood looking at the dome pieces.

"In time for what?" asked Bob.

"Oh, nothing Bob!" replied Wendy, hurriedly.

Soon the first layer of the dome was complete. Wendy decided to sneak away to make the phone calls about the party.

"Wendy, what do we need to do next?" asked Bob.

"Just look at my notes," called Wendy. "It's all in there!" And then she zoomed away on Muck, leaving Bob looking confused.

Wendy arrived at her mobile home and found the Bentleys there.

"I'm just calling Mrs Percival," said Mr Bentley.

"Oh, I'll talk to her," said Wendy, nervously.

Just then, Farmer Pickles arrived with everyone from Bobsville, including Mrs Percival! Wendy was worried that Bob might see them.

But Wendy and Muck had to go back to the site.

"You get back to the dome and we'll sort out everything for the party," said Mr Bentley.

"Oh no, I can deal with it," said Wendy. "Don't do anything, Mr Bentley. I will be back soon."

At the site, Wendy soon saw that Bob hadn't left space for the doors into the dome!

"Oops, I'll just have to start this layer again!" said Bob.

"But that will take too long!" said Wendy.

"Wendy, why don't you let Mr Bentley organise the party?" whispered Muck. "You can't organise the dome and the party at the same time."

Just then, Scrambler zoomed in with Mr Bentley.

"Oh, Mr Bentley, I'm sorry I wouldn't let you help," said Wendy, looking at Muck.
"Can you organise the party?"

"I would be delighted!" replied Mr Bentley, and Scrambler zoomed off!

With the team working together, the dome was soon finished. Bob went to his mobile home to get some cordial to celebrate.

But when he returned, the dome was decorated with balloons and everyone was wearing party hats!

"Surprise!" cried the Bobsvillagers.

"I don't believe it!" said Bob. "Wendy, when did you manage to organise all this?"

"I've had lots of help!" smiled Wendy.

And then everyone cheered, "Hooray for Sunflower Valley!" as fireworks exploded.

THE END

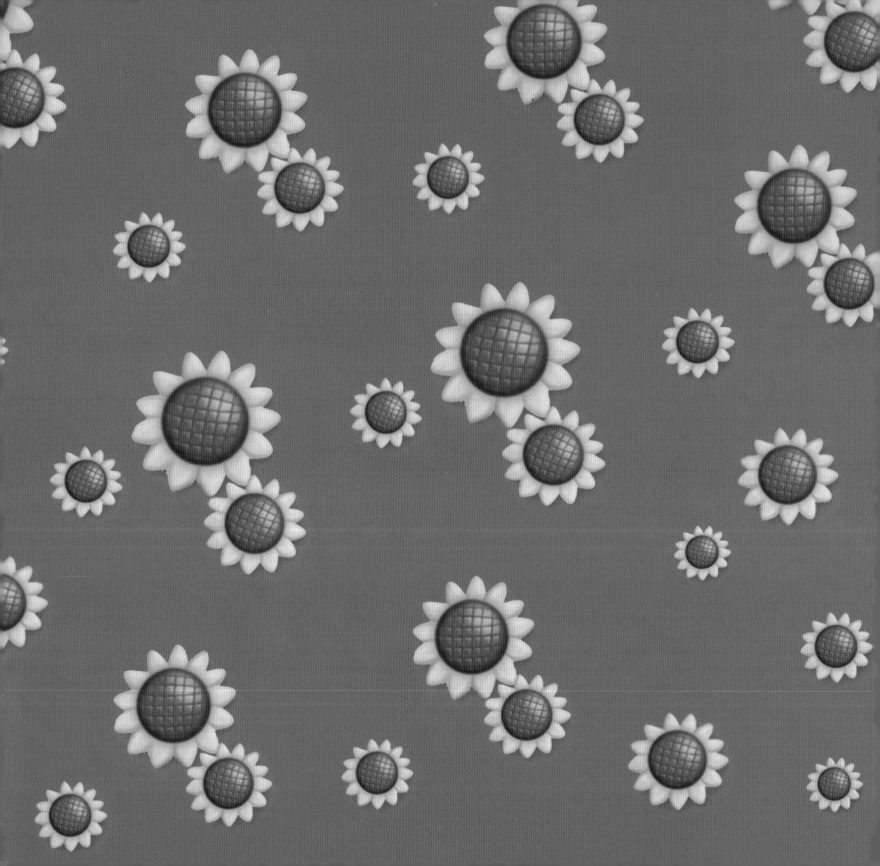

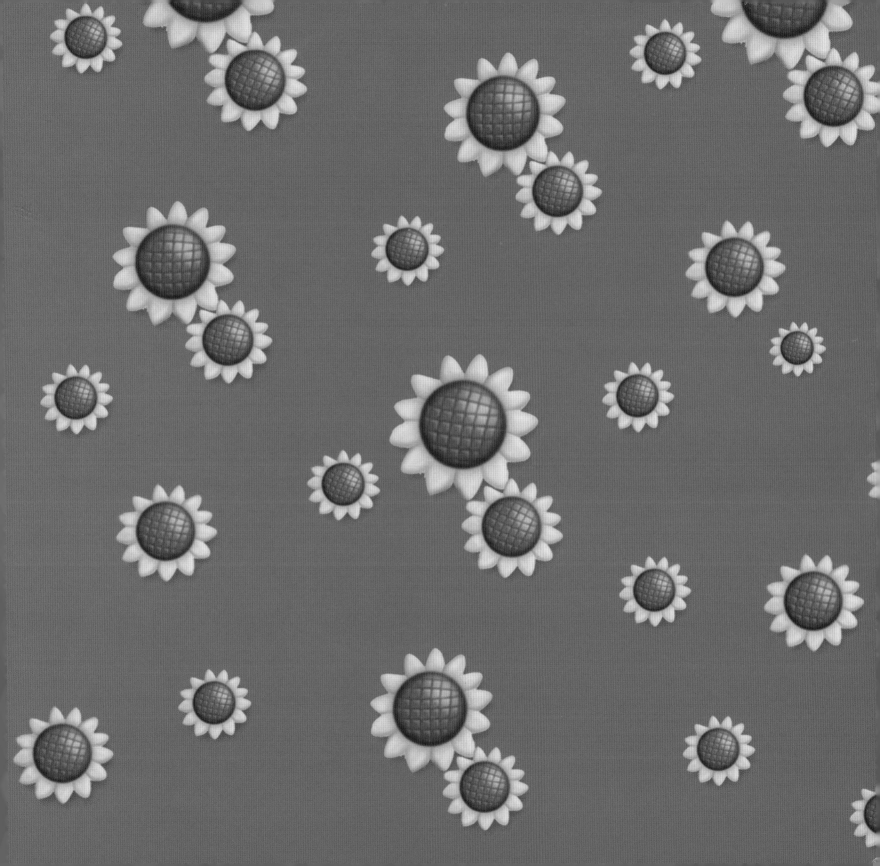

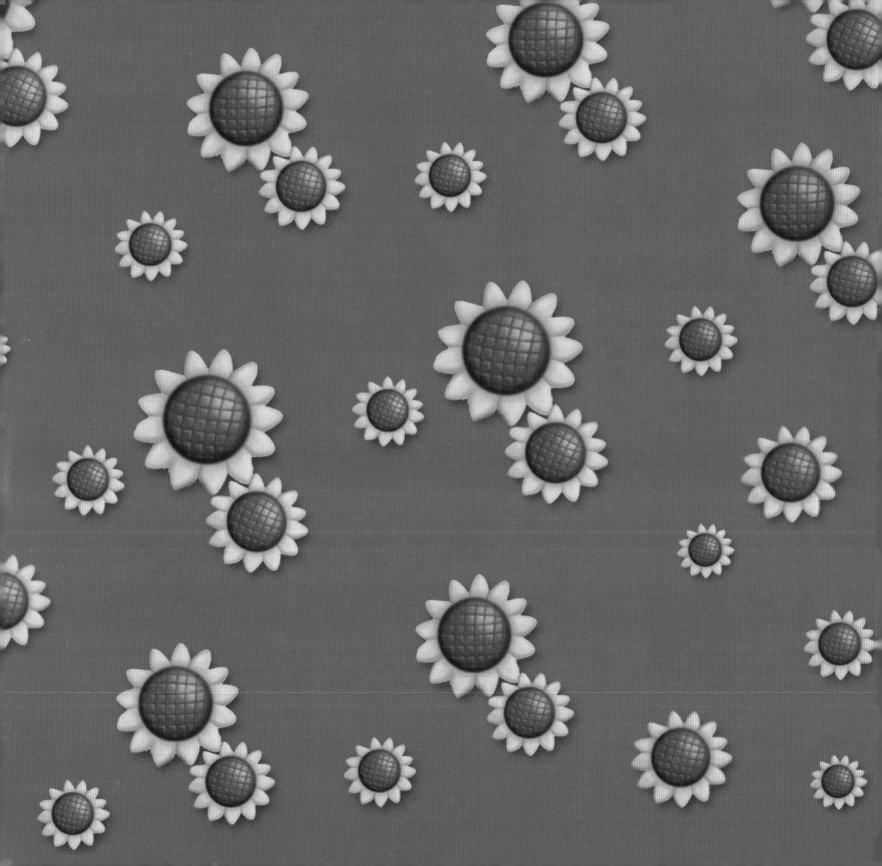